Back in the Game

'Back in the Game'

An original concept by Jenny Jinks

© Jenny Jinks

Illustrated by Zeynep Özatalay

Published by MAVERICK ARTS PUBLISHING LTD

Studio 11, City Business Centre, 6 Brighton Road,

Horsham, West Sussex, RH13 5BB

© Maverick Arts Publishing Limited November 2020

+44 (0)1403 256941

A CIP catalogue record for this book is available at the British Library.

ISBN 978-1-84886-729-1

www.maverickbooks.co.uk

This book is rated as: Lime Band (Guided Reading)

Back in the Game

Written by Jenny Jinks

Illustrated by
Zeynep Özatalay

Chapter 1

"Leo, can you get the washing in please?" Leo's mum called.

But Leo barely heard her. He was just about to complete the very last level of Danny Dangerous, the most epic computer game Leo had ever played! He just had to catch all the Crazy Critters. These were little blue balls of fluff that were running and hiding all over the place.

Then Leo would be the ultimate champion! Finally he spotted it—the very last Critter!

"Leo! Now!" Mum shouted, making Leo jump.

"Coming," Leo sighed, pressing pause on his game.

He ran outside and grabbed the washing off the line. Thunder rumbled in the distance.

Suddenly, a bright flash of lightning struck overhead. It looked like it had hit the house! Leo darted inside.

But when he got back to his game, the screen was empty. No Crazy Critters. No Danny Dangerous.

Nothing. Leo pressed play, but nothing happened.

"Oh no," groaned Leo. That stupid lightning strike! Now he would never get to finish the game.

Then Leo spotted something scuttling across the floor towards his open door. Leo blinked.

It couldn't be, could it?

He jumped up and peered out. It was! A real-life Crazy Critter was running down his stairs!

Chapter 2

Leo raced after the Crazy Critter, and he saw

even more of them zooming along the corridor

towards the kitchen. Leo didn't know how this

could possibly have happened, but he knew he

had to do something about it quickly, before Mum

and Dad spotted them.

He crept after them into the kitchen. *Oh no!*

thought Leo, peeking inside. Mum and Dad were

both in there. They were going to spot the

Critters for sure!

Luckily, Mum was busy making lunch and Dad

was reading the paper. They had no idea an army

of little Crazy Critters had just invaded their

kitchen. Leo spotted some climbing up the table

leg. One was swinging from the fridge.

You can do this, Leo told himself. It was just like a level of Danny Dangerous. Only this time, Leo was the hero.

One of the critters was getting dangerously close to Dad. Leo dived at the table, grabbing the Critter, but knocked the sugar bowl to the floor.

CRASH!

"What are you doing?" Dad said, looking up from his paper. Leo stuffed the Critter in his pocket just in time.

"Sorry, I tripped. Don't worry, I'll clear it up," Leo said quickly. Then he spotted another Critter speeding towards the sugary mess on the floor. Leo scooped it up and put it in his pocket with the first one before anyone could notice. He swept up the mess, while secretly searching the kitchen for more Critters. Then he spotted one.

Oh no, Leo thought. It was on Mum's head! And it looked like it was just about to jump into the pot of soup on the stove.

Without thinking, Leo leapt across the room in a single bound. Everything felt like it was in slow motion. He reached out and scooped up the Crazy Critter, just as it was about to dive, swatting Mum's head in the process.

"Ouch!" Mum cried. "What's got into you?"

"There was a bee in your hair," Leo said, thinking quickly. "It's gone now. Flew out of the window."

It was then that Leo saw it. The window was wide open. Outside, he could just make out a line of small, fluffy, bright blue things bouncing away through the long grass.

Oh no! Some of the Crazy Critters had

escaped!

Chapter 3

Leo made a dash for it. He grabbed his rucksack from the hall. He would need something bigger to put the Critters in. The ones in his pocket were wriggling like crazy.

Luckily, the storm had gone away again, just as quickly as it came. Leo rushed outside. He was running around the corner of the house when he bumped headfirst into someone running in the other direction. SMACK!

Leo fell to the floor. When he sat up, he found himself face to face with...

"Danny Dangerous?!"

"Excuse me, I'm on a highly important mission," Danny said, jumping up and dusting himself off. "You haven't seen any Crazy Critters running around, have you?"

"You mean like these?" Leo said, proudly showing Danny the three he had caught.

"Oh, well done," Danny said. "I've caught two. That makes five. So there are still five more out here somewhere to catch."

Leo sighed. Danny would probably want to complete the mission on his own. After all, he was the hero of the game. It was his job to catch the Critters and save the day.

"Well, come on then, let's not hang about. We have to find them!" Danny said.

"Really?" Leo said excitedly. "I can help?"

"You seem to be an expert Critter Catcher. I could use someone like you on my team," Danny said.

Leo grinned from ear to ear. He was going to help Danny Dangerous. This was the best day ever!

Chapter 4

"What's this?" Danny asked for about the hundredth time since they had left the house. "What does it do?"

"That's a daisy," Leo laughed. "It's a flower. Well, a weed, actually. It doesn't really do anything."

"Amazing," Danny said, as if daisies were the most fascinating things in the world.

"Can we get back to tracking the Critters now?" said Leo.

Danny seemed to have forgotten their urgent mission. Everything was distracting him.

"Oh yes, sorry," Danny said. He looked down at the Critter Catcher 5000. "This says they are just up this road. We can go down this secret

passage and surprise them."

"That's not a passage, that's the sewers!"
Leo laughed. "Trust me, you don't want to go
down there."

"Oh, are you sure?" Danny shrugged.
"Alright, well, we'd better get a move on then.
They appear to be just up this hill."

Leo could hear music up ahead. Bright, multicoloured lights flashed from over the hill. Leo spotted a poster. There was a town fair on the green. Today. Leo looked down at the Critter Catcher 5000 and gasped.

"Oh no," he said. "I know where the Crazy Critters are going!"

Chapter 5

Leo and Danny rushed towards the green. It was packed with stalls and stands, games and rides. Now that the sun had come out again, loads of people were out enjoying the fair. Leo looked around. Finding the Critters would be like looking for a needle in a haystack.

"Maybe we need to split up," Leo said, turning back to Danny Dangerous.

But Danny had disappeared.

Oh no! Leo thought. Now he had lost the Critters *and* Danny.

Then Leo spotted Danny. He was gazing longingly at a sweet stall. Leo rushed over.

"Come on, Danny, we need to go."

Danny pointed at a pot of giant gobstoppers.

"We can get some later..." Leo began.

But then he saw it. In the middle of the pot was

a Critter, happily munching its way through a giant sweet. Yes!

"Can I help you?" the man on the stand asked.

"Can I have a scoop of giant gobstoppers please?" Leo asked.

The man scooped a heap of sweets into a paper bag. The Crazy Critter was hidden right in the middle.

"And a couple of these super long wiggly things. And those bright twirly things too," Danny said excitedly. *He's probably never had sweets before*, Leo thought. *Poor him.*

The man scooped up lollipops and jelly snakes while Leo said goodbye to a chunk of his pocket money. Once they were safely away, Leo pulled the Critter out, still munching a gobstopper, and put it safely in his backpack. The others jumped up, fighting hungrily over the huge sweet.

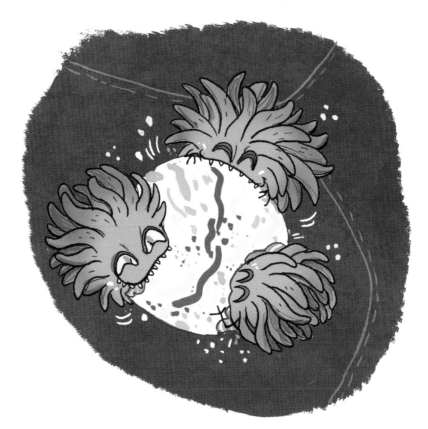

"That's it!" Leo said excitedly. "The Critters love sugar!" That's why they had gone straight for the sugar bowl in his kitchen. And why they were fighting over the gobstopper.

"Of course!" said Danny.

Now they knew just where to look. They ran from the sweet stall to the donut stand, and from the candyfloss stall to the ice cream van. Leo might have run out of pocket money, but they soon found all the Critters, stuffing their faces with all the sweet things they could find.

"We did it. We've got them all!" Leo cried as he shut the last Critter safely in his backpack. But that still left him with one problem. How were

they going to get them all back inside the game?

And why did Danny Dangerous look so worried?

Chapter 6

Suddenly Leo heard the thundering of heavy footsteps. A giant shadow loomed over them.

Oh no! thought Leo, for the hundredth time that day. There was always a big boss to beat at the end of every level.

The Gobbling Goblin came crashing towards them, gobbling trees and bushes in his way.

"We need to do something. Fast!" Leo said as the Gobbling Goblin knocked down stalls and sent people running.

"Pass the sweets!" Danny Dangerous called.

"This is no time for a snack!" Leo said.

"Trust me!" Danny said. Leo stuffed a couple in his pocket for later, then threw the bag to Danny.

"Hey, Goblin!" Danny shouted. The Gobbling Goblin stopped gobbling and peered down at Danny. "Chomp on something your own size!"

Danny crouched down low. Leo knew exactly what he was going to do. He had seen this move loads of times—Danny was going to try to double jump! Didn't he realise he wasn't in the game anymore? It was never going to work.

But as Danny jumped up, Leo could tell that something was different. Danny was going higher, and faster, than any jump Leo had ever seen. It was working!

"Epic!" Leo whispered under his breath.

Danny flew through the air. He threw the bag of giant gobstoppers straight into the Gobbling Goblin's huge open mouth. The Goblin chewed

hungrily. But then he stopped, confused. The sweets had glued his mouth shut! The Gobbling Goblin couldn't gobble anymore!

But the trouble wasn't over yet. The Goblin thrashed around angrily. He stomped on tents and swiped at rides, causing chaos and destruction wherever he went.

"He's out of control!" people screamed.

This was a disaster! They had to stop him. But how?

Chapter 7

The Gobbling Goblin was on the rampage. If only they had a rope... Then Leo remembered what was in his pocket. But he was saving them as a treat for later... No, this was an emergency.

Leo pulled a jelly snake out of his pocket. He made one into a lasso, swung it round his head, and caught the Gobbling Goblin in one swift flick. The Goblin's arms were tied. But his legs were still stomping clumsily.

"Danny, catch!" Leo pulled out the second jelly snake and threw one end to Danny Dangerous. Danny took hold of the head, and with Leo holding the other end, they ran towards the Gobbling Goblin. The Goblin stumbled into the jelly trip wire. The boys ran round and round the Goblin's legs until he was completely tied up. He fell to the floor with an almighty CRASH, broke into a thousand tiny pixels, and then disappeared right in front of their eyes.

"We did it!" Leo said, high-fiving Danny. "We defeated the boss. I completed the game!"

Leo looked inside his bag, just in time to see the Critters all disappearing too. But that meant...

"You're going to leave now too, aren't you?" Leo said to Danny.

"Yes," Danny said. "But I have a feeling we will have adventures together again someday."

And with that, Danny Dangerous bent down and double jumped up into the air, and disappeared.

"Epic," Leo whispered.

★★★

There was lots of talk about what had happened

at the town fair. Some said a robot had gone on a rampage. Others thought that a parade float had gone astray. One person was even sure that aliens had landed from outer space. Only Leo knew the truth.

For Leo, life went back to normal. He missed having his computer game to play. He never got it working again. Not that it mattered. He had managed to complete the game in real life, and made a friend in the process, and that was a million times better. But Leo missed having Danny around.

Then one day Leo was walking back from the

sweet shop with a bag of super long jelly worms, thinking how much Danny would have enjoyed them, when he spotted a poster that made him stop in his tracks. Danny Dangerous was smiling down at him. A new Danny Dangerous game was coming out next week! Leo grinned. It looked like he might get to see his friend again sooner than he thought!

Discussion Points

1. What caused the Crazy Critters and Danny Dangerous to be released from the game?

2. Who was the big boss Leo and Danny had to defeat at the end of the story?

a) the Thundering Troll

b) the Gobbling Goblin

c) the Wicked Witch

3. What was your favourite part of the story?

4. What did the Crazy Critters love to eat?

5. Why do you think Danny Dangerous was so distracted by things like daisies?

6. Who was your favourite character and why?

7. There were moments in the story when Leo had to be **the hero**. Where do you think the story shows this most?

8. What do you think happens after the end of the story?

Book Bands for Guided Reading

The Institute of Education book banding system is a scale of colours that reflects the various levels of reading difficulty. The bands are assigned by taking into account the content, the language style, the layout and phonics. Word, phrase and sentence level work is also taken into consideration.

The Maverick Readers Scheme is a bright, attractive range of books covering the pink to grey bands. All of these books have been book banded for guided reading to the industry standard and edited by a leading educational consultant.

To view the whole Maverick Readers scheme, visit our website at

www.maverickearlyreaders.com

Or scan the QR code to view our scheme instantly!

Maverick Chapter Readers
(From Lime to Grey Band)